In loving memory of my *grand*fathers
Mack Little and William Robert Jones
— *Eloise Greenfield*

For Kelvin Keith Gilchrist, a wonderful father.
And special thanks to little David Horton.
— *Jan Spivey Gilchrist*

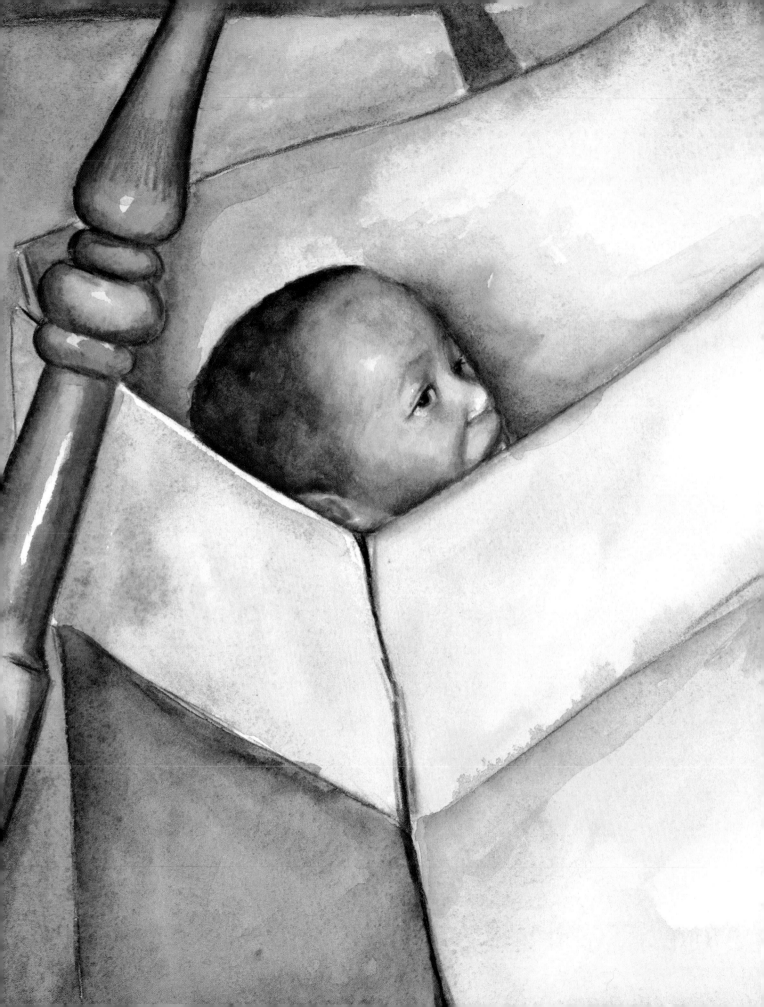

FIRST
PINK LIGHT

BY
Eloise Greenfield

ILLUSTRATED BY
Jan Spivey Gilchrist

Published for Black Butterfly Children's Books
by Writers and Readers Publishing, Inc.
P.O. Box 461, Village Station
New York, New York 10014

in England:
c/o Airlift Book Company
26/28 Eden Grove
London N7 8EF

Library of Congress Cataloging Card Number 91-072C48
cloth ISBN: 0-86316-207-X
trade ISBN: 0-86316-212-6
2 4 6 8 10 9 7 5 3
Text first published in the Harper & Row editions 1976.

Illustrations in gouache and pastels

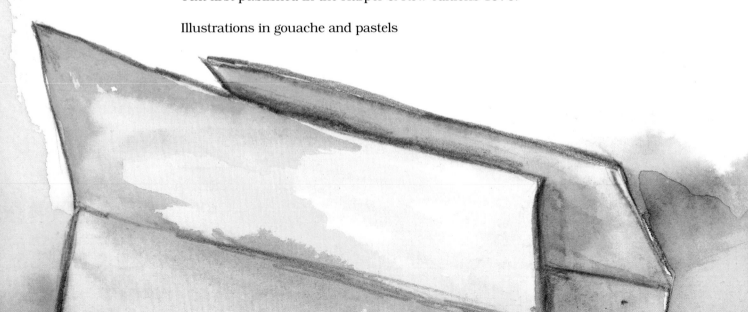

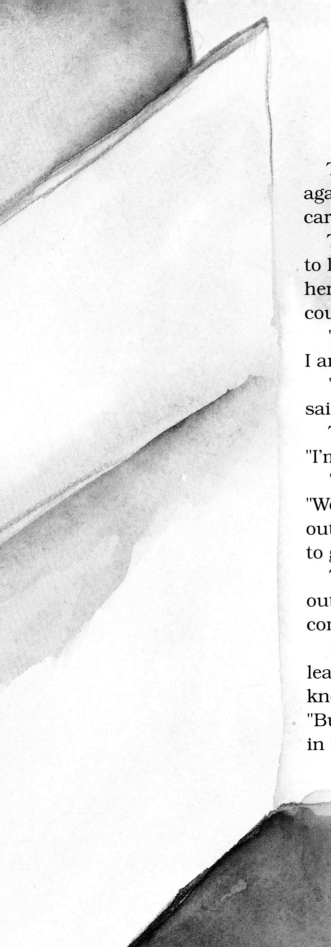

Tyree leaned the last piece of cardboard against the legs of the chair and looked at it carefully to be sure it was standing just right.

Then he crawled under the chair and tried to look out. He couldn't see his mother doing her homework on the table, so he knew she couldn't see him.

"Mama," he called, "you don't know where I am."

"Where in the world are you?" his mother said. "Are you lost?"

Tyree laughed. "No, I'm not lost," he said. "I'm inside my hiding place."

"Oh, you are, huh?" his mother said. "Well, in just one minute you have to come outside your hiding place. It's time for you to go to bed."

Tyree laughed again and stuck his head out. "Mama," he said, "you forgot! Daddy's coming home! I can't go to bed yet."

His mother put her pencil down and leaned her arms on the table. "Now, you know I didn't forget that, Tyree," she said. "But your daddy won't be home until early in the morning."

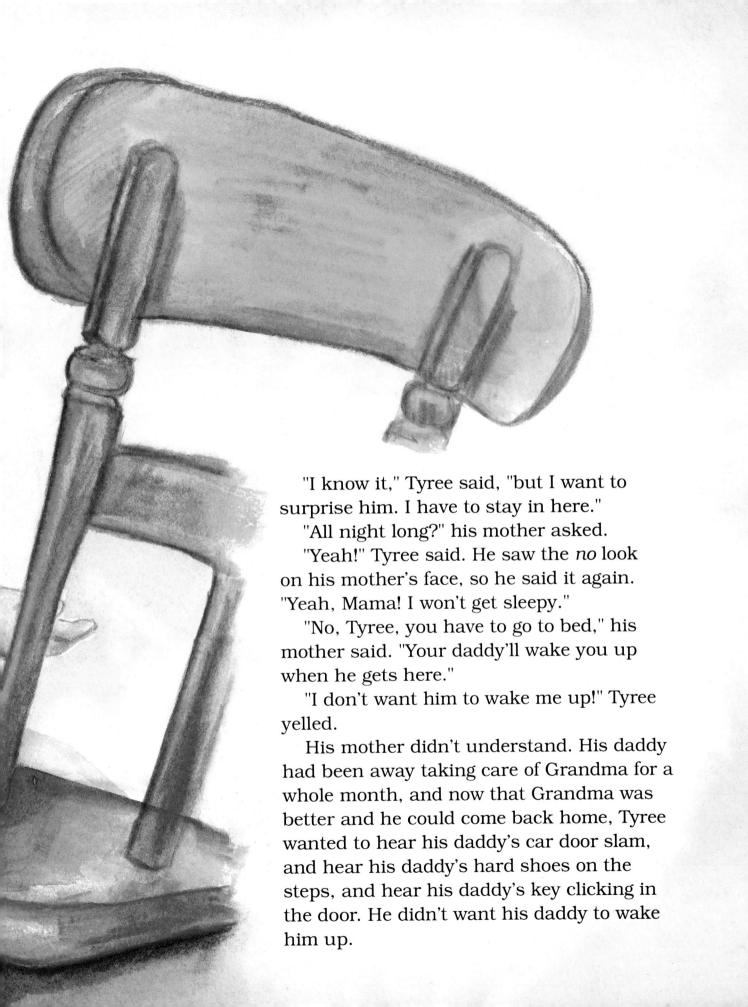

"I know it," Tyree said, "but I want to surprise him. I have to stay in here."

"All night long?" his mother asked.

"Yeah!" Tyree said. He saw the *no* look on his mother's face, so he said it again. "Yeah, Mama! I won't get sleepy."

"No, Tyree, you have to go to bed," his mother said. "Your daddy'll wake you up when he gets here."

"I don't want him to wake me up!" Tyree yelled.

His mother didn't understand. His daddy had been away taking care of Grandma for a whole month, and now that Grandma was better and he could come back home, Tyree wanted to hear his daddy's car door slam, and hear his daddy's hard shoes on the steps, and hear his daddy's key clicking in the door. He didn't want his daddy to wake him up.

He crawled out of his hiding place, and a piece of cardboard fell down. His mother was making him mad, and she was making him break up his hiding place, too. He sat down hard on the floor.

"I can't go to bed!" he yelled. "I have to wait for Daddy!"

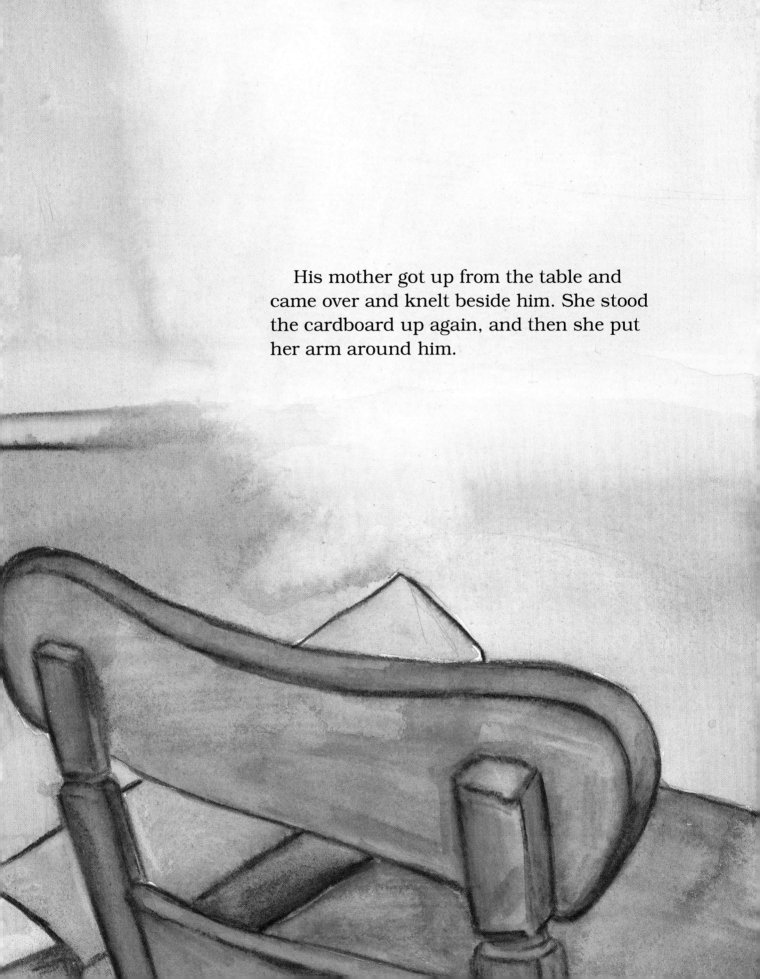

His mother got up from the table and came over and knelt beside him. She stood the cardboard up again, and then she put her arm around him.

"Now, listen, Ty...," she said.

Tyree knew he had won, then. He always won when she said, "Now, listen, Ty...," in a soft voice like that. He stopped looking mad and made his face real, real sad.

His mother looked at him hard, and then she looked at him soft, and then she said, "Okay, I'll make a deal with you. If you put on your pajamas and sit in the big chair, you can stay up. Then, when it's almost time for your daddy, you can hide."

Tyree looked at his hiding place. "I won't know when it's almost time," he said.

"Yes, you will," his mother said. She took both of his hands and pulled him up. "Come on over to the window, and I'll show you. Now, look at the sky. Right there, over Mr. Walker's house. What do you see?"

Tyree cupped his hands around his face so he could see better. "Nothing," he said. "Just dark."

"Well, when it's almost time, you'll see something else," his mother said. "Because every morning, just before the sun comes out, it sends a pink light out first. So you can sit right here and watch, and when you see the first pink light, it'll be time to hide. Okay?"

Tyree thought for a minute. "Okay," he said. "That's okay."

His mother leaned over and pointed to her
cheek, and he gave her a loud kiss. Then he
ran to his room and put on his pajamas fast,
and came back and jumped into the big
chair.

"Why don't you get your pillow," his mother said, "so your head won't get tired?"

Tyree got his pillow and put it behind him in the chair. Then his mother said, "I bet your blanket would feel pretty good right now."

He got his blanket and wrapped up in it, and it did feel good. His mother was right.

He looked over at her. She was back at the table, and she was frowning. But he knew it was about the homework and not about him. He had won, but she wasn't mad.

He looked out at the sky over Mr. Walker's house. As soon as he saw the first pink light, he would get inside his hiding place. And when he heard the key in the door, he would call his daddy and keep calling him, and his daddy would follow his voice and find him. Tyree laughed, thinking about how he would jump out and into his daddy's arms.

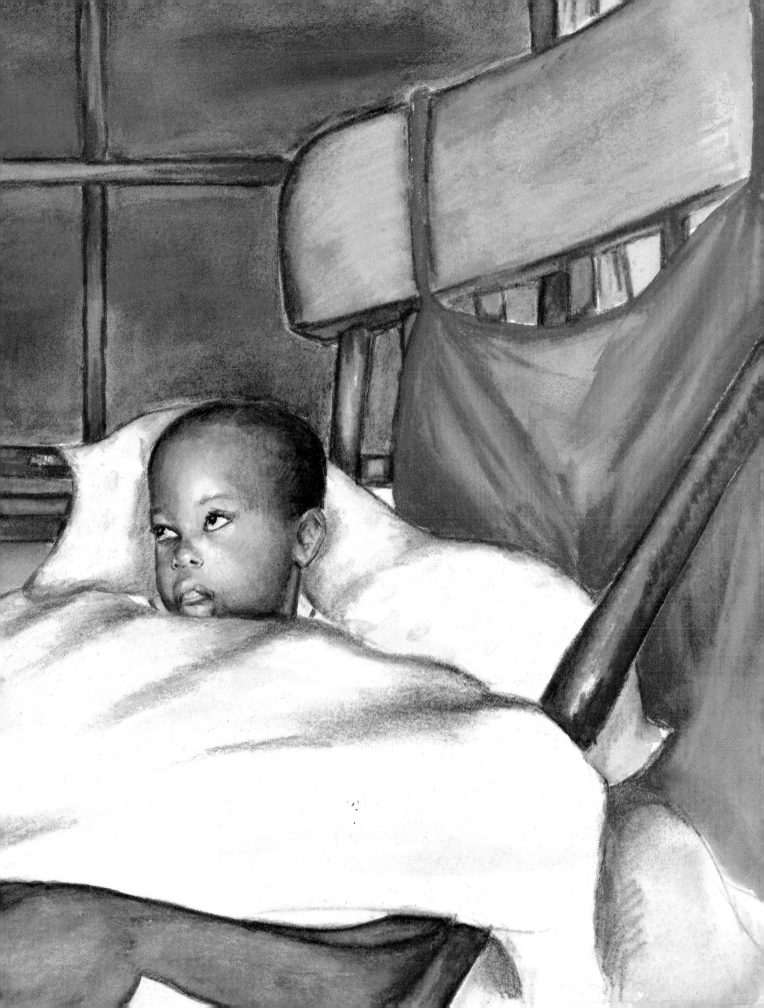

He leaned his head back on the pillow and stared at the sky for a long time. And the pillow got softer, and the blanket got warmer, and just before he felt his eyes close, he knew his mother had won. But he was too sleepy to care. He smiled in his sleep.

Tyree wasn't awake when the sun
stretched its first pink light across the
sky. And he didn't hear the key clicking
in the door,

or see the man with the strong brown face
when he stood beside him and looked at him
for a long, long time.

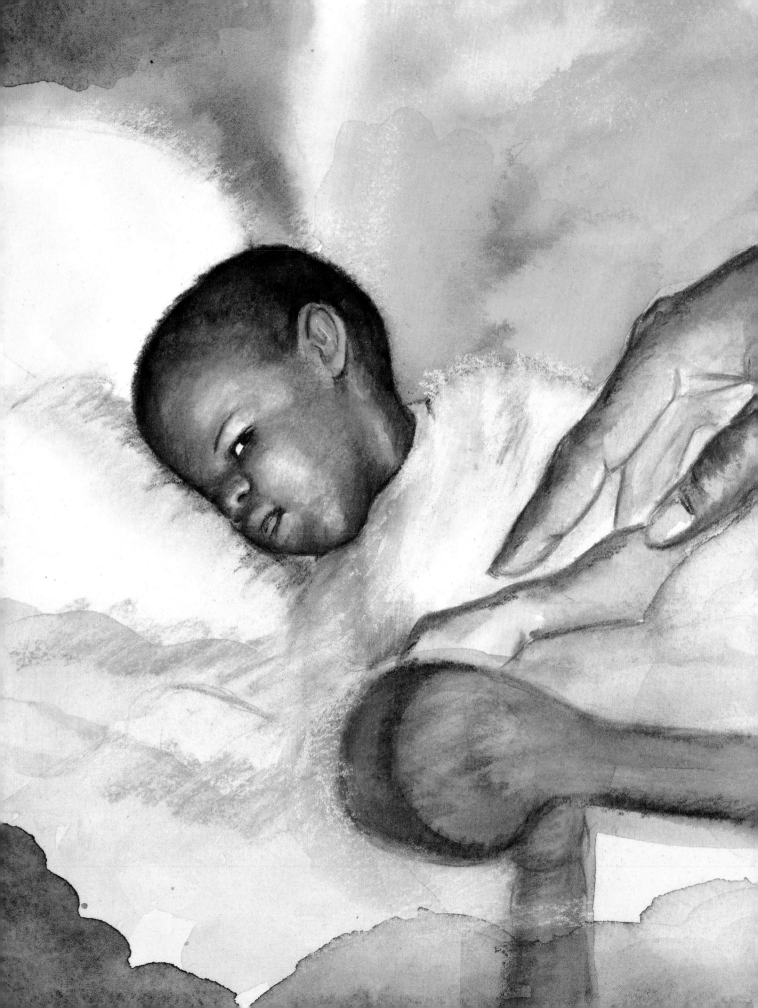

He didn't wake up until he felt a big hand on his arm. And even then he didn't wake all the way up.

All the time he was reaching out to hug his daddy, and his daddy was holding him real close and carrying him to bed, all the whole time that he was wishing his daddy would never, ever, have to go away again, Tyree never even opened his eyes.